# TH
# BLACK WOLF

To Lily
Love.
Elizabeth x

# THE
# BLACK WOLF

## ELIZABETH LAWRENCE

Daisa
PUBLISHING

The Black Wolf
First published in Great Britain in 2022 by
DAISA PUBLISHING
An imprint of PARTNERSHIP PUBLISHING

Written by Elizabeth Lawrence
Copyright © Elizabeth Lawrence 2022

A CIP catalogue record for this book is available from the British Library.
ISBN 978-1-915200-28-0

Book cover design by: Partnership Publishing
Book Cover Image © Shutterstock 341426492, 1531055951

Book typeset by:
PARTNERSHIP PUBLISHING
North Lincolnshire, United Kingdom

Partnership Publishing is committed to a sustainable future for our business, our readers, and our planet; an organisation dedicated to promoting responsible management of forest resources. This book is made from paper certified by the Forestry Stewardship Council (FSC) an organisation dedicated to promoting responsible management of forest resources.

We operate a distinctive and ethical publishing philosophy in all areas of our business, from our global network of Authors to production and worldwide distribution.

A fantasy book written by Elizabeth Lawrence
for her teenage grandchildren

Dedicated to
My mum

# CONTENTS

# PROLOGUE

## NEW BEGININGS

Alpha Julius and his Luna Organza lay asleep in a makeshift bed among the remains of the pack house and the pack buildings they had just battled so hard to claim for themselves. There was little remaining of the pack that had battled alongside them and nothing of the pack they had attacked.

The lone wolf saw the smoke and devastation from afar, he knew instantly that destruction of his pack was inevitable, as soon as he got close to the site to be able to see what was happening. Slowly, he edged himself into a small gap between the hedgerows. Patiently he waited till nightfall.

Gradually, he came out from his hiding place and

stealthily moved towards the now flattened remains of his once beautiful home. He moved so silently that not even the dead would be disturbed.

As he moved toward the remains of the pack house, he saw exhausted warriors asleep, realising that the two that should have been on guard had also given way to their exhaustion.

Silently and swiftly, he moved forward. This cannot have been their only attack these few days to be this tired, he thought. Wolves have extensive energy levels. It was then he saw the head of his father with his mother, almost bitten in half as she reached out for him.

He was crushed, filled with a pain like no other. Pain turned to anger, then to fury as amongst the ruins of the pack house lay a man and a woman who exuded power and energy.

Instantly the wolf knew these to be the Alpha and

the Luna of the pack.

In one swift move of anger, he reached out with his mouth and grasped the Alpha's neck, breaking it instantly. At the same time, his claw slit the throat of the Luna almost taking off her head. He then turned and ran as fast and as far as he could...

# CHAPTER I

## ANARCHY

**The year was 2052.**

The earth had been ravaged by a war that had begun back in 2020. The year the people were suppressed; uprisings followed, governments overthrown, and millions of people died. And as the fighting continued, the earth began to take exception and have a battle of its own.

Earthquakes began to happen all over the world - some big, some not so big; with lots of land taken over by tsunamis.

Volcanic eruptions and other natural disasters followed as a consequence. It was about this time that the human race discovered what some of them already knew... *we were not alone* on this planet of ours. Creatures that we considered fantasy were in fact real and living under our very noses and had been since the beginning of humanity. Which brings us closer to where we are now.

The UK and most of the UK's east coast had had a real battering, destroying much of the coastline. Those that had survived thus far moved inland to safer havens; though some smaller battles remained over territory and various petty things, the earth was settling into relative peace.

Among these now at peace was a young man, a very strong young man, who went by the name of Michael. Michael was a werewolf; he was hungry, his body and his powers were weak, *he needed to eat*. He had long since forgotten how far he had come and how long he had been walking. Sure, he could have run, but that would have left scent all around

- it was easier to simply use his wolf to hunt and nothing else.

He knew he was almost where he needed to be, he could smell it in the air, it felt familiar despite the fact he had never been there.

Michael walked through the trees, his heart beating loudly. He felt almost deafened by the silence.

There it stood in all its glory… **the house**. It was everything that Michael thought it would be and more, though it needed work *and lots of it*, he wasn't afraid of work.

Apparently, his father had been driving along the road and caught a flat, and this kind man had helped him. Together they had replaced the tyre and the gentleman had offered tea and sandwiches. His father had so loved the house and talked about it a great deal through Michael's childhood.

This was going to be one tough job to execute, the house was much larger than he had anticipated. He was strong, he could source the materials and what he couldn't source he could make. He had money but there was no one to pay for these properties, they were mostly dead.

Michael settled down for the evening, ate his food and made a makeshift bed in one of the rooms.

He rose early the next day, feeling fresh. He was delighted to realise that the water from the floods had only reached the top of the road - as the village was built in a dip, it had taken the biggest hit. He realised that he would be able to salvage a good bit of the materials he needed for the house from some of the damaged cottages and other buildings.

Michael had done much thinking and since the village had no name that was of any meaning to him, he chose to name it Lupos.

It was still very quiet, and he looked around the house hoping to find something resembling a kitchen. Luckily for him there was an old-fashioned Aga oven so he knew he could light that, collect wood and cook on it later, but for now, a light breakfast would do.

# CHAPTER 2

## MICHAEL AND EZRA

Breakfast done and thoughts running around his mind, Michael allowed himself to stretch and as he did so, he immediately heard his bones begin to crack. He breathed in deeply, as each and every bone began the process of transitioning from a human skeleton and muscle to that of a wolf. In the blink of an eye, he stood proud and softly padded out of the room into the open air. This majestic, caramel-coloured wolf that he had transitioned into was indeed something to behold.

Michael was now Ezra; he had allowed his wolf to totally take over, his human form lay hidden deep inside his wolf, just as his wolf would lay deep inside his human form when the transition was the other way around.

Although it may seem like they are separate entities, Michael and Ezra were one and the same, although human was always the dominant. If one died, the other died. It was like having a soul that could come alive and take over in animal form and talk to you via telepathy or 'mind link' as the wolves called it.

As Ezra turned from the house, his face caught the breeze and he mind linked to Michael, *'hold tight.'* He was going for it like never before, and together they ran until totally breathless, exploring their surroundings and getting a couple of rabbits for food later on.

Michael's mind was relaxing. He felt free. The two of them breathed in the air, they were going right over the fields and there was absolutely no sign of anyone at all. Michael and Ezra barely spoke except to say to one another that this was definitely a 'safe' area, and one they could make a place to settle into.

After approximately ten miles, Michael suggested they turned back and move slowly towards home. Ezra agreed and he slowed to a steady gait, turning back in the direction of the house. Some two miles in, Ezra came to an abrupt halt. Wolves having excellent hearing can pick up sounds from quite some distance away. He had heard something, but Michael realised there was no fear attached, *caution* but no fear.

Michael heard it too, a whimpering - it sounded human. Ezra needed to track this sound and Michael needed to work with him. The sound was not close, Ezra pricked up his ears and held his nose in the air. There was no smell to be had yet, the whimpering was louder to the left where the ditch was. About 200 yards. Ezra could smell it now, it got stronger and about ten yards from the hedgerow, Michael came to the fore and asked Ezra to pull back and allow him to transition into his human form.

Michael shifted back and as quickly as he could, he put the joggers on that were tied to his leg. It was no time at all before Michael found the source of the whimpering.

Tucked into the undergrowth were two little girls, both around the age of 4 and seemingly terrified. Michael picked them up gently, and softly spoke to them, assuring them that all would be well.

After being initially afraid, both girls settled into his arms, and he carried them back to his home. *It would be nice to have some company*, he thought.

The girls, it turns out, were twins and their names

were Hala and Aremis. Now, as much as Michael loved their company and would enjoy having them around, he needed to know where they came from. After all there was no sign of anyone around and neither child would talk to him apart from giving him their names.

And so, time passed, days to weeks to months and finally to years.

In this time of peace there had been no sign of anyone, just the three of them. The house was finished, and Michael's mind turned to thinking about finding his mate. The moon goddess ensures that the wolf has a mate; they are drawn to each other. At the age of 18, most werewolves find their mate almost immediately, however, in these unusual times, it was not so easy.

# CHAPTER 3

## SISTER SECRETS

Three years had passed in the blink of an eye; Hala and Aremis talked nonstop through mind-link, but they had put a block up against Michael hearing them. He of course knew there was more to finding the girls than met the eye. In the world of werewolves, *nothing* happens without reason.

The three of them had become like a small family, the girls called Michael 'Papa Alpha,' and the two girls had become strong under Michael's care, learning much about the culture and the old ways of the werewolf.

Aremis loved to sit and listen to the stories and over time became very educated, loving the library.

She was a little bookworm and very sensitive.

Hala shouted to Aremis, "come help me sister, we have dinner to cook," and they set about dinner, just the two of them in silence to the world but full of chatter to each other.

Hala, it seems, was the more confident one and the stronger of the two. Michael had worked hard to ensure the girls were taught how to behave correctly and as a result, both were lovely natured girls with good souls.

"Hala, do you realise we are only one year away from getting our first set of powers?" said Aremis.

"Yes," Hala replied. Hala continued, "we won't be leaving here, we will be a part of the Lupos Pack. That is our destiny."

Aremis looked at her sister slightly confused. "But how are we supposed to keep this from Papa Alpha, we were ordered not to reveal anything until our secondary powers come at 14!"

"Aremis, we will have to be very careful. When our father left us there in that hedgerow, he knew Michael was in the area, he *knew* he would hear us. Michael was chosen very carefully, and you know that. If they had survived the battles, we would have known by now. We must accept that Michael is our guardian. Mother's spirit will guide us when the time is right," remarked Hala.

Aremis conceded, "yes, you're right." She smiled, "you're always right, sister dear."

Aremis and Hala settled back into life and waited to see how Michael was going to deal with the issue of finding his mate; as their time was yet to come.

# CHAPTER 4

## FULL MOON

Michael sat alone in the library. He been around all the houses and nearby properties to collect every book he could, and now sat in what could only be described as a substantial library, covering almost every subject you could think of - thanks to the secondary school that was no longer in use.

He questioned what he was going to do. He couldn't leave the girls and *wouldn't*. He would have to send out messages via mind link to any werewolf, sorcerer or being that could receive his message within a reasonable radius.

The problem with that, Michael thought, would be rogues. Then he laughed, practically *no one* had a pack right now. Technically, they were all rogues.

Michael consulted Ezra. *'Hello my wolf. What should I say? Help me, I'm lost?'*

Ezra stirred and let out a whimper, he was tired as they ran and trained every day. He liked to rest in the afternoon.

Michael laughed as he felt him stretch and think, then mind link him. *'Ah my friend, split the area up into sections,'* Ezra said, *'and wait for a day or so between each time you send out your message - it's the only way at the moment.'*

And so, Michael sat and began to clear his mind to send out a message to the first area. He continued with this for several weeks and *nothing*. Disappointment filled his soul.

*'There cannot be anyone within that radius, I need to widen the radius and widen out my search.'* He

reached for the one of the books on the shelves; it was a local map book, a very handy little affair, rescued from a fuel station. He sat down and plotted out his new radius. It was about this time that the girls popped and said their goodnights.

Michael decided to leave anymore work till tomorrow, *the moon was full.* He checked on the girls who were now sleeping and decided to let out his frustrations with a good run.

The still of the night was filled with the sound of cracking bones, and as the moon shone down, the beautiful caramel coat of Ezra glistened.

Once again, Alpha Michael was a magnificent wolf. He was bigger now and much more muscular. Ezra ran with such speed that Michael was once again able to relax his mind. They were heading in the direction of the old silver mine but would be going round it, not in it. Silver is poison to a wolf.

They had no sooner gone 6 miles when Ezra lost his footing, and the smell of vanilla and honeysuckle filled his senses.

Both Michael and Ezra said at the same time...

'*MATE.*'

# CHAPTER 5

## LUNA

*MATE. MATE. MATE.*

Michael's head was shouting, Ezra was as giddy as he could be, jumping around and Michael seemingly had no control over him.

The scent was all consuming. There, right in front of him lay the most beautiful girl he had ever seen. She was a werewolf for sure, but there was something else he couldn't quite put his finger on.

She was hurt, it appeared to be just her leg. Michael immediately felt her pain, his own body feeling drained of energy, (mates always feel each other's pain, although it is ten times less). Michael struggled to contain his feelings. He leaned forward, having already changed to his human form, and using all his strength, he went to pick her up. As he did so, the familiar sparks appeared on both him and the mysterious lady. Michael felt a warm feeling shoot through his body, knowing this woman was to be his true mate.

However, many other things come with having your true mate. Michael felt a sharp pain in his leg, the same as his mate. It was bearable, but if it held discomfort for *him*, he knew she was feeling it ten times worse. He was still strong, and though he felt her pain, he picked her up in his arms bridal style and carried her as swiftly as he could to the house.

Although Michael and the girls had worked hard on the house and had built a small hospital, it only had beds and the basic equipment. Although he took her there, he wasn't really sure what to do. Michael was a very intuitive werewolf and so on his way to find this place he had taken the time to learn many things. His knowledge was vast; he cleaned the wound and there was nothing to see, but she appeared to be getting weaker.

'What is it? What is it?' Michael thought; he just couldn't see anything.

The wound appeared clean. He looked further into it and could see nothing. He tried to mind link to connect with her wolf… he could hear the wolf but had no communication. Michael himself didn't feel like he was on full power either.

Michael checked her body and there were no marks at all. It *has* to be the wound. He went back to the injury, just then the girls came in with water and towels.

"Why don't you go for a drink and freshen up, Papa Alpha?" they said. "We will watch until your return." He nodded in agreement and as he left, the girls got to work immediately; they may not have their basic powers yet, but these girls were gifted.

Hala touched the wound.

"There's a slither of silver right under the muscle in her leg." Aremis said immediately. "Michael won't have felt it as he is too close to her, and he will be heady with the sweet smell of her. He won't be able to think straight. We must remove it quickly; pass the knife, I'll get it out before he returns."

As the girls worked quickly and the silver was removed, there was an almost immediate difference in her condition. The wound did not need stitches as a wolf heals very quickly, so the leg was bandaged tightly to hold the wound together for the next 24 hours, by which time it should be fine. Both girls washed and dressed the lady in a clean gown. As they finished, they looked at one another, then at the lady and with a knowing glance, they left.

# CHAPTER 6

## LUNA GAVENIA

Gavenia lay there, her body healing now the silver had been removed. As she lay there, her thoughts drifted to the moment he had found her.

Gavenia had left her pack, she was a Luna and as yet did not have an Alpha to lead the pack with her. She and her pack needed a safe place to make a home. She had no idea what had drawn her here, especially as it had been her intention to head further north to their original home.

What Gavenia hadn't realised, is that at some point in recent history, a silver mine had been discovered. She had felt its presence but had assumed she was safe as it was boarded up and clearly untouched for some time. Normally, she would never have crossed it as it would have been tempting fate, but it was nightfall and she was looking for somewhere to lay her head, so wanted to take short cuts where possible. Her gut took her over this way.

However, as Gavenia was walking at a fast pace across the mine, she slipped and felt something pierce her leg. Her powers were immediately weakened, and while she had enough energy left, she teleported by mind to a place of safety. She pulled the silver from her leg but felt no better and immediately fainted.

The next thing Gavenia knew was her wolf calling her and whimpering 'mate.' Gavenia could smell him, musky, a delicious combination of oranges and ginger. She breathed it in, not daring to open her eyes as she felt herself being lifted into his arms.

Although she was weak, she felt the sparks between them and a rush of warmth throughout her body. *Gavenia was safe.*

As she lay there in the bed, she kept her eyes closed at all times, listening to every conversation. She was growing weaker by the hour.

Michael continued to work on her to try to make her well, she felt his frustration - Gavenia heard him speak of his disappointment in himself. The sparks of attraction were there but not as strong; Gavenia knew she couldn't help, it would take her energy and she simply couldn't afford that right now.

Then suddenly, voices pierced her thoughts; girls, *young* girls. She could hear their chatter and she knew that her mate, this man they called 'papa' could not. She found this strange. The girls stopped their chatter, they knew that this beautiful lady could hear them.

Once the silver was gone, Gavenia was able to tune into the girls and knew they were good souls. And so, she stayed this way, healing her body until Michael's return.

As she remained there, she could only hope that Michael would not reject her. Oh, she had beauty, that's for sure, with her jet-black hair and pure silver streak, her diamond blue eyes and a figure to die for. Waiting was not one of her best points. Gavenia was feeling very impatient anticipating Michael's return.

The doors opened and she could smell that altogether wonderful essence of orange and ginger and sure enough, her wolf started doing somersaults inside her.

'*Calm down,*' Gavenia spoke to her through mind link. Paz sat wagging her tail, waiting. Gavenia's heart was beating wildly, waiting for his touch. Michael slowly stroked Gavenia's arms and sparks flew around the room as he touched her forehead and gently kissed her.

Gavenia could hold back no more. Her eyes shot open as Michael's golden orbs started in shock, as he looked into a pair of bright red eyes...

*Vampire.*

# CHAPTER 7

## ACCEPT OR REJECT

Michael turned and left the room immediately, his body filled with pain.

*She was his mate, how could he reject her*, he thought. He sat in the living room, his head in his hands. His whole body was in pain, and he knew he wouldn't be the only one that would be feeling it. His mate was aching from his denial. She had to do *something*; she couldn't lose him.

Abruptly, the room was filled with the smell of her essence, vanilla and honeysuckle. Michael turned and as he did, he inhaled as there before him she stood.

"Hello, Alpha Michael James McKenzie, I am

Gavenia Estrella Allanach." She spoke, her red eyes filled with unshed tears. Michael felt her pain. As she spoke to him, she explained how she came to be there. Her voice was like honey and Michael felt a warmth and peace fall around the room. In that very moment he was captivated, and he knew there would be no one else.

"I left my pack to find safe haven for us to stay, I was somehow drawn this way. It seems we are to be mates. You are an Alpha, a pack leader and I... I am a Luna, and my pack are not too far from here. I have contacted them; they are on their way. It will take a few days for them to arrive. I am hoping they will be welcome, Alpha."

Gavenia had given him such a lot of information in such a short space of time, that Michael felt somewhat overwhelmed. He just stood there his mouth agape. He had no words. Every time he saw

Gavenia, he felt pulled, he wanted to take her in his arms and kiss her... he still felt confused by the vampire eyes.

'*Michael*,' Gavenia spoke through his thoughts, '*we need to talk this through.*'

"Err... y-yes," Michael replied, "we do," and once again Gavenia cut through his mind, informing him that she was going for a run first.

All at once, the crack of bones sounded and where Gavenia had once been, stood a beautiful black wolf with a strip of silver down one side. The eyes were still red, Michael noticed, but before he could comment, she was gone in a flash, leaving Michael totally bewildered.

Gavenia was running like something possessed; she needed blood... after all, she was a vampire, but did not practice on humans. There was lots of wildlife out here and so she caught and took a small drink from each, *too much and it would die.*

Once she had filled up, her eyes returned to the beautiful blue that everyone loved. It did not take away the pain she felt from Michael's lack of acknowledgement, the very same pain that Michael felt right now. He was torn. He knew there was never going to be another that he felt like this for, but could he get over the vampire issue?

Gavenia was back at what would now be known as the pack house. Once dressed, she made her way to Michael. He was sat in the vast lounge area, his head down, when the smell hit him like a wall. He once again inhaled deeply the familiar vanilla and honeysuckle scent. Looking up, Gavenia stood before him, with the most beautiful blue eyes he had ever seen, with flecks of white that twinkled like diamonds. Michael held the gaze, and he knew he could not reject her.

# CHAPTER 8

## THE PACK

"Gavenia, you are right, we need to talk," stated Michael. "Shall we go to the library? I'll get the girls to bring us refreshments… is that part of your diet?" he said, with a half-smile.

Gavenia wasn't sure how to take the last remark, but went to the library and sat opposite Michael in one of the beautiful leather chairs. She began the conversation as she felt she had the most to say.

"Michael, I know that the years of war and destruction have taken its toll on the earth and its beings, there is less land now, and so many less beings to live here. The majority of our packs were destroyed and those of us that remain have wandered the earth alone. I knew of you Michael from the past, before I was able to detect my mate. I know you're from the north of Newcastle, and that your parents were killed in a lengthy battle over land. Your pack was destroyed and fortunately for me and you, you weren't there that day. I know this, because it was a pack that at the time was well known to me."

Gavenia continued her tale, her soft voice drawing him in, like music to his ears. Michael listened intently to what she had to say.

Continuing her story, Gavenia explained to him what her pack was made up of.

"So, to finish Michael, you will understand that we have a few from here, a few from there etcetera, and we have turned our backs on some of the old ways and traditions. We need you to help us move forward as a pack. We are something of a mixed bag for a pack, Michael: there are werewolves, vampires, sorcerers, witches, and humans. Hybrids too. We all live together in harmony. The one thing we are missing is a strong leader to organise us, schedule training and most importantly, work towards one goal. I have worked *hard*, and the pack has come a long way. I need you Michael, I need you to help me to finish the work."

For some time, Michael had sat listening to her, lost in the melody of her voice and the beauty of her eyes, and she had no sooner finished her sentence than he was up, and lifting her toward him. He kissed her hard on the lips... she was his.

"Tell me, Vena, you have vampire blood in you, you feed as a vampire, but you run and transition as a wolf. I'm curious as to why this might be," he asked of her. Gavenia was keen to give him all the information he wanted and was quick to reply.

"Obviously I am dominantly werewolf, which is why I transition as such, but the vampire blood runs in my veins and compels me to feed it, there is no other way I can answer." Michael could no longer hold back, he accepted her as his Luna *and* as his mate.

Paz and Ezra were both going crazy.

"I shall from this moment forward, call you Vena."

The girls came running in. "Yeah Papa, I thought you'd never do it!"

And so, it was Gavenia, and Michael. Hala and Aremis began to get the place in order to welcome the newbies to their world. They had two days to make at least four houses respectable.

Aremis was put in charge of the kitchen and food. They had four bathrooms in the pack house and each of the eleven bedrooms was ensuite. Extra towels were laid out and the banquet table filled;

Aremis had finished her tasks and walked over the old road to the row of houses.

"Wow! Papa, Vena, Hala! You've done a great job, come get cleaned up before their arrival."

"Indeed, yes," responded Vena, "they're about an hour away, we must hurry."

No sooner had they all washed and eaten, a somewhat rushed affair, then there was a knock at the door. They all looked at each other, the girls giddy and excitable.

Michael had to be calm and in control with an air of authority; he went toward the door and opened it.

There before him stood a very handsome, very tall man. Michael was left in no doubt that the man who introduced himself as 'Baldasorre' was a vampire.

# CHAPTER 9

## A WELCOME PARTY

Michael felt overwhelmed and nervous, he wasn't used to this. Gavenia touched his back and he immediately felt calmer.

Baldasorre sensed his hesitancy and stepped back with a bow. Recognising what he had done, Alpha Michael nodded gratefully in his direction, and the two immediately felt a bond.

From the slightly higher view of the steps, Alpha Michael James addressed the pack.

"Welcome, I see that you are tired and hungry, so I won't keep you long. Please, for the benefit of myself, I wonder if you would separate into groups for me." Almost as soon as he said it, there before him stood five groups: sorcerers, humans, hybrids, werewolves and vampires. Alpha proceeded to designate the houses to the latter of the five groups, leaving only sorcerers and Baldasorre and his family facing him. He had asked that once everyone was cleaned up, they should return to the pack house, preferably within the hour.

Alpha then turned his attention to Baldasorre.

"I sense you are not only strong, but your greeting showed empathy. You will be my Beta; your home is the pack house. Hala, take Baldasorre and his family to the west wing. Aremis, please take these gentlemen and ladies to other available rooms until we have houses for them. Oh wait!" Alpha Michael stopped them, "where are the witches!"

He was met with laughter, huge roars of laughter that made his cheeks burn as anger ran through his veins, but the sorcerers just walked on, and one rather elderly looking one smiled and winked at him.

Gavenia could feel his anger as she walked towards him.

"Hey, don't be cross. They're not laughing at you, more at the situation. The witches are here, they've been here all time. I couldn't come with no protection. They arrived the day you found me."

Michael was not happy and as he turned from Gavenia, he was met with eleven witches... *stunning* witches. Even the elderly ones were beautiful. They looked towards Michael and bowed in reverence whilst swishing their wonderful capes around them.

He had thought the capes would be black, but they were beautiful rich colours, embroidered with all kinds of symbols. The oldest and by far the most stunning was named Hilda. She greeted him and thanked him for the care he had shown Gavenia.

Alpha bowed in return and took his Luna's arm, walking inside.

Under his breath he hissed, "don't ever make me look a fool again!"

Gavenia realised that Michael would accept nothing less than one hundred percent.

How would he react when he knew the truth of what she had done?

# CHAPTER 10

## FIREWORKS & MAGIC

The party was in full swing. Everyone was dancing, the humans and hybrids were playing instruments, and the vampires were showing off their flying skills. They picked up the children and swirled them round. There was a huge fire; the sorcerers were working together with the witches to provide entertainment by way of fireworks and magic. The whole affair was really something to behold.

The bold black wolf watched in the distance, he would bide his time, *which was something he had plenty of right now*. In a swift movement, he turned and ran into the distance. He was far enough away to not have his fragrance smelled and he'd been close enough to see what was happening. He had seen what he needed and would work with that in mind.

Alpha Michael and Baldasorre took the time to get to know each other to watch the pack, survey their behaviour, and how they work as a team. Once they were satisfied with what they saw, it was time to establish a boundary.

Whilst the party continued, Michael mind linked Gavenia and told her of his plans. She agreed and Michael changed to the now familiar caramel wolf, and Baldasorre swished his magnificent cape. Before you could blink, soaring above Ezra was the most magnificent shiny black bat.

For a split second Baldasorre's bat who went by the name of Luca, (bringer of light), could have sworn he saw something in the distance of his peripheral vision but no, as he turned to look there was nothing. And so, off they went. Deep into the night to mark the pack's boundary.

Hilda the Head Witch walked steadily towards the Luna. She smiled, and as if she had slipped into her thoughts, she said, "I think Aremis would be easiest, and you need to separate them."

Gavenia was shocked, she turned to look at Hilda, "was you reading my mind?"

"Yes, I was, you must learn to close off, it's dangerous," replied the witch leader. Hilda and Gavenia looked at one another, and something passed between them. They both held their gaze, unaware of the gaiety surrounding them, when suddenly a firework exploded right over their heads, making them jump. The crowd roared with laughter, and Hilda and the Luna Gavenia laughed in return.

It had been several hours now, and the party was

drawing to a close. Baldasorre and Alpha were back; Michael loved Vena dearly, and as he watched her bringing them drinks and party leftovers, his heart was aching to take her in his arms and make love to her... to feel her soft, warm flesh against his, and to kiss her neck where he had bitten her to make her his.

Vena was now marked as all mated wolves should be. Michael's thoughts were drifting but business must come first.

In the meantime, Hilda was waiting for Gavenia in the office. As Gavenia walked toward the office door, her mind was twisting in every direction. She opened the door to the office and sat down, they regarded one another for a moment before Hilda spoke.

"I believe I know what the girls are, but there's something else Gavenia. *There's a mist that hides their true identity.* I've tried everything I can think of to get through," spoke Hilda. "We have to separate them. It's the only way..."

✦

# CHAPTER 11

## SECRETS OF THE PAST AND FUTURE

The pack village was really beautiful. It was independent of everyone; they built generators, they built shops, the village dip was now a swimming lake with trees and flowers. They grew their own vegetables. Life felt good right now.

The humans played a huge part in this. Their knowledge was insurmountable. *We wouldn't have done nearly as well without them*, thought Alpha Michael.

Alpha and his Beta Baldasorre had agreed to form a council. The council would meet once a week in the village hall. At the last meeting, it had been raised about each individual group having a time out to honour their old traditions. Much thought had gone into this and Alpha and Baldasorre were still thrashing it out. So much so that Gavenia had had enough and told the two of them to take a hard run, or fly in Baldasorre's case.

Without realising it, Luna Gavenia had just given herself the opportunity to split the girls and get Aremis to talk. Gavenia checked outside. With the boys gone and kitchen duties to do, this could prove easier than she thought. She walked into the garden and the girls were there playing with a few others, *mostly hybrids.*

"Aremis," Gavenia called, "would you mind helping me please, I'm a little behind with lunch."

She looked up with genuine joy and said, "of course Vena, you know I love to help!"

Aremis followed her mistress, Vena, into the

kitchen, and began helping out. In the corner of her eye, Gavenia could see Hilda watching curiously. Hilda had blocked Hala; she was busy and shouldn't notice.

"Aremis," said Vena, "are you ok?"

"Yes, of course I am," came the reply.

"Then tell me sweetie, what are you? I need to know; I can't help you if you don't tell me."

"No," she cried, "please," and immediately became very defensive. "Vena, don't make me say it." Her eyes were full of tears and her cheeks were wet.

"Please," Vena begged, holding the crying child to her chest. Gavenia thought for a moment, putting herself in the child's shoes. Secrets are tough to keep. *She ought to know…* she was holding a secret that could blow her relationship with Michael apart.

Aremis was still crying and softly but firmly, Vena pushed the child to speak.

"I'm not supposed to tell Michael," she sobbed.

"And you're not, you're telling *me*, and I promise not to tell him," assured Vena.

"Really?" Asked the young girl.

"Yes, *really*," Vena repeated.

Gradually, Aremis spoke softly to Gavenia, relaying the whole story as best she could.

"I come from Ireland, that's where I get my black hair and green eyes from. There was such destruction where we lived; earthquakes, huge waves, and fighting every day. My mother was afraid for us. So, my father teleported us and we came to the hedgerow, but my father knew Papa Alpha was in the area, and so he left. They said they would come for us just as soon as it was all over, but they never have, so we think for sure they have been killed."

"Aww my love, I'm sorry," whispered Gavenia.

"You have me and Papa Alpha. We can help you! Now just tell me what you are, and I can help."

"Vena," Aremis sighed as she looked into her mistress' eyes. "I trust you, but you *must* promise to keep my secret."

"I promise" answered Vena.

"We are both witches. Our powers are strong already and in two months on our eighth birthday, we will get our junior powers and knowledge of our elements."

"Don't worry little one, you will be fine," vowed Gavenia, and ushered her outside. Hilda erased her recent memory, so that Aremis had no recollection of the last half hour.

# CHAPTER 12

## THE COUNCIL MEET

Hilda looked at Gavenia and asked if she knew how many witches made a coven.

"Why, thirteen of course," confirmed Gavenia confidently.

"That's right," approved Hilda... "and how many do we have?"

"Eleven, oh dear you are sho...rt," she said, as the realisation dawned on her that Hala and Aremis made thirteen.

"Did you also know that witches aren't assigned to an element?"

"No," answered Gavenia. "I didn't know that, with all the fighting there was so little time for school."

"I shall help you with this," retorted Hilda. "Only two beings that I know of are gifted to elements: sorcerers and Fae. I'm sure that they are not sorcerers, Gavenia. It has been known for Fae to join a coven if they have witch blood. They are Fae, they have fae magic, witch blood, combined with an element which we have no idea of yet. Let me tell you, these girls are very powerful indeed."

Gavenia went pale and was frustrated with her lack of knowledge. It was soon to be their birthday so plans would have to be made. In the meantime, Michael and Baldasorre, not having come to an agreement, were sitting in the library, mulling over their thoughts. Luna Gavenia entered with refreshments and an idea that all three could agree on.

The council meeting was scheduled for two pm at

the village hall. One member from each group was there, with Alpha Michael and Beta Baldasorre at the head. Everyone was seated and the doors opened, then in walked Luna Gavenia. She slowly took her seat at the opposite end of the table and apologised for her lateness. The meeting was called to order.

"First to speak today is your Luna Gavenia, if you would my love," said Alpha Michael.

Standing, Gavenia addressed the room.

"There has been much talk of wanting to have time out to teach your own kind the old ways. Whilst we empathise with your feelings, we do not want to take anything away from the pack. The pack works well together."

Before she got another word out, they were shouting and looking from one to another, banging the table. Gavenia looked towards Michael, but he said nothing, so she let Paz out just a little. The room went quiet, as Paz let out a deep rich throaty growl.

"Well ladies and gentlemen, now that I have your attention again, let me explain our intentions. One of the large barns in the pack grounds is currently empty. We shall work together to make good of the barn and extend. Please, look at the board for plans. Everyone, and I mean *everyone*, with only two exceptions, Alpha Michael and Baldasorre, will attend our new school. We all lack knowledge about ourselves and each other. The elder from each clan will be a tutor, this way we all learn together. The two exceptions will have private lessons."

The elders asked for a moment to discuss this. They all sat in silence while they talked through linking minds, and they all agreed it was a good way to make sure the old ways were not forgotten.

Luna made sure she concentrated her studies around witchcraft and vampires, but in her spare time tried to find out as much as she could about fae, their folklore and their elements.

# CHAPTER 13

## 2056 BIRTHDAY WISHES

The whole pack was buzzing with the news that the girls were having a party; everyone loved them, they were such lovely young things, always smiling and never speaking ill of anyone.

Gavenia decided she would have to get the boys out the way for the night so she arranged a boys camping night, bonding, so he wouldn't be there to see the first party.

*Only she and Hilda could see that one.*

The boys had left, they would be back tomorrow by the time the party began. Supper finished and movie watched, the girls went to bed not knowing what might lay ahead.

Gavenia and Hilda sat back, eyes closed, listening to the clock ticking. Suddenly the lounge area felt small, and Gavenia went to sit on the step for a while. She was awakened by Hilda shaking her softly by the shoulder.

"Gavenia," she said, "we must go, it's about twelve, it's almost time."

The two of them climbed the stairs quickly and placed themselves on the floor between the girls. They had no sooner settled, and it began.

The girls both began mumbling and moaning, their bodies convulsed, and it was evident that they were in some pain, and yet they remained unconscious.

The heat was oppressive, and the girls were wet through with sweat. As the pain grew stronger, their mumblings grew louder, and it was then that Gavenia and Hilda realised that they were not saying the same thing. The auras that surrounded both girls were different colours too. Gavenia wanted to take away their pain, but Hilda assured her that the only thing that she could do was hold onto a hand as she was doing, as it would comfort the child knowing someone was there to help.

After about half an hour, an enormous sound erupted from their bodies, followed by white lights in every direction. Tiny little stars filled the room and slowly settled before vanishing. Silence followed, and the room was still.

Unexpectedly, it was like the earth had risen from underneath their feet and as it rose, the colours came. They swirled around and as if drawn to a magnet, a bright green fog tinted with yellow surrounded Aremis. Once again, the colours swirled around but this time they were drawn to Hala, and she was surrounded by every colour of blue imaginable.

The colours stayed for some time, and during that time, energies could be seen circulating the girls' bodies, sparkling when it reached the head and hands.

This was not unusual to Hilda, but Gavenia was in awe of the spectacle before her. After a couple of hours, it was all over. The girls looked exhausted, and they slept deeply and heavily.

Hilda looked to Gavenia, who was still sitting there in absolute awe of what had just taken place.

"Vena," she prodded, "the elements... did you see them?"

"Yes, I think so," she replied. "Was it the colour of the auras that make up the elements?" Hilda asked.

"Yes, that's right. It is White for Air, Red for Fire, Blue for Water, and Green for Earth. So, the twins are *water* and *earth*. I am happy with these elements as the sorcerers will be able to work with these."

Gavenia and Hilda slowly and quietly walked from the room in silence.

# CHAPTER 14

## SPELL CHAOS

Gavenia had just finished the girls' breakfast; she had figured it would be a good idea to give them some rest after the previous night.

Just as her feet hit the first steps to their room, there came the sound of banging and clattering. The girls' squeals met her ears, and she ran the last few steps to the girls' room where she was greeted with disaster.

Both girls were crying and shouting, every time they moved their arms something new happened, *chaos was an understatement.*

Gavenia had already called for Hilda through mind link, and she wasn't far behind her. Hilda erupted into glorious laughter that filled the room. Vena looked to her for support, but none was forthcoming, and the chaos continued. As it continued, the laughter grew. Vena was furious, she turned to Hilda and demanded she help at once, knowing full well the boys would be back soon. There was water everywhere and twigs and leaves… it looked like a forest dumping ground with toys floating around, wet through.

Hilda had laughed till she hurt. "I was expecting something of the sort," she explained as she immediately cleaned up and blocked the girls' fae powers.

"Now girls, today will be a busy day, off you go, get your breakfast. We must not let Papa Alpha be aware of any of the goings on from last night."

Everything was clean and tidy. It was like nothing had happened and no one was any the wiser.

Preparations for the party had begun; the kitchen was a hive of activity and everywhere you looked, someone was doing something that was going to make the party a special affair.

All the girls had been making fine dresses from whatever fabric they could find, and of course that had included Hala and Aremis. They wanted something very special.

Vena had worked every day now for several weeks to ensure they both had the most extravagant looking white dresses. Each was now decorated with ribbon in the colour of their element.

Michael and Baldasorre were both back now and speaking to Gavenia in hushed tones.

"Yes, yes, we will have the party but from now on we will have a border patrol. We cannot afford to rest on our laurels and assume it is safe out there."

"...Yes Vena, we were camping, but there was

definitely the odour of a rogue. I say rogue because he didn't make himself known to us. He had been on our land recently, but as we searched there was no further evidence to suggest he was still within our borders; however, I feel unsettled. And therefore, we will address the pack tomorrow with our concerns. In the meantime, there are patrols in place..."

# CHAPTER 15

## THE BLACK WOLF

From the top of the peak that overlooked the village, the lone black wolf lay quietly, watching. He had the perfect view of the packhouse from this position. He was close to the pack border but far enough away to not be seen or smelled.

He had been very careful and now he watched with this amazing sight that he had been gifted with.

The party went ahead as planned; the whole pack was present with the exception of the border patrol. Hala and Aremis enjoyed all the attention that was bestowed upon them. They were more than aware that part of their secret would have to be revealed this very night, but most would remain buried in their souls, until the time came when they could open up and tell the world *who* and *what* they really were.

There was nothing but merriment and happiness as the music played and food was eaten. Everyone had the most amazing time, and the party was almost at a close when Gavenia and Hilda halted the proceedings to make an announcement.

Vena spoke first. "Good evening everyone, thank you so much for coming, and thank you for all the wonderful gifts you have given our lovely twins! Michael, please come stand by my side," she proclaimed. "The girls and I have something to tell you, and the rest of the pack. Hilda, perhaps you could help me out here?"

"Yes, of course," replied Hilda.

"As everyone knows, I have waited patiently for two more members for our coven. We are eleven and not the thirteen that we should be. I need look no more; they have been here all along. I give you Hala and Aremis..."

The crowd erupted. Everyone was overjoyed that the twins had at last got some kind of identity. Even Michael, who was mildly annoyed that he wasn't the one to find this out, was too happy to be angry.

The coat of the black wolf was shiny in the moonlight. He was proud of the way he looked and the way he had looked after himself.

His beautiful eyes glistened as the moonlight shone right into them. He had seen everything; *the Luna had a pretty good set up going on here*, he thought. He needed to think how he would deal with all of this. The one thing he hadn't thought of was that the Luna would have so many around her, and a mate. Although he had thought there might be a strong possibility of a mate when he mulled over the circumstances, he had hoped there wouldn't be. Still, this was not a problem, just a challenge that could be overcome.

With thoughts of revenge on his mind, he slowly rose and took himself off to the makeshift home and as he did, he shifted back to his human form. There was now no need for the wolf, he'd had his run early this morning and didn't need to use his long sightedness that he'd been gifted. He simply needed to rest for now, to sleep and make his plans.

He had plenty of time and he knew he *must* be patient.

# CHAPTER 16

## BORDER BREACH
*Six months prior to the girls' 14th birthday*

The guards on the border patrol were becoming complacent. There was no one around and they were getting bored of the same kind of thing every day. So, when head guard Teddy mind linked them all to say there had been a breach on the west side of the border, all the guys got a little jumpy. Within minutes, the rest of the pack were at the site whilst several members went over to the north, south and east as a precaution. Some of the pack warriors stayed at the village to protect the children, meanwhile, the witches and sorcerers placed spells to protect everyone.

Thankfully, it turned out that this was all unnecessary, but their organisation showed how well their training had paid off.

Alpha Michael and Baldasorre approached the western boundary and could see the patrol guards, stood over a young man approximately twenty yards ahead of them.

"All this for one man…" smirked Baldasorre. Michael returned his smirk, but they both recognised the seriousness beneath. They walked up to the man and the guard. The mysterious man was very tall; he had a shaved head and dark green eyes, and seemingly worked out and trained to keep his body in good shape.

Michael asked him if he was wolf, to which the man replied that, yes, he was, but he was having problems transitioning since losing his mate. His mate had died giving birth and the pup had died alongside her. Although werewolves always give birth in their human form and give birth to human babies, the babies are referred to as pups by their parents.

"And what brings you to these parts?"

"My mate and I were looking for somewhere safe to settle. It has been two months since she passed, and I just carried on walking and looking for somewhere that might be a good place to stay."

"Alone with no wolf is not a good idea in these unsettling times…" Baldasorre advised Michael to accept him into the pack temporarily, until the next council meeting when a decision would be made as to whether he could stay or not. So, it was that Ciaran was taken along to the pack house to be fed. The pack kept a small self-contained unit next to the pack house for situations just like this and Ciaran would have a guard for the time being. He would be guarded until Alpha and Baldasorre were both satisfied he posed no threat to anyone in the pack or to the pack itself.

Gavenia had been down at the schoolrooms with the children while this had happened. She was in no hurry to get back home to the pack house; there was plenty to do here for now, so when the girls were due to leave for the day, she would be leaving with them.

Vena still marvelled at how much they had grown and how far they had come with their powers over the last few years. They were well ready to accept their full powers in six months, and from there they would develop their skills separately, according to their elements.

No sooner had she finished the last of her inventory, than the girls were at her door ready to go home, giggling and laughing as they popped their heads round to check if she was ready. Vena was, and together the three of them walked towards home to get the tea ready for the four of them.

They went in the back way and as they got into the kitchen, Vena heard a familiar voice and her face paled. *NO! NO! NO! it couldn't be, not here! What was he doing here?*

She didn't leave the kitchen, instead she peered through a crack in the door just in time to see a guard escort her brother out of the pack house...

# CHAPTER 17

## BLOOD AND WATER

Gavenia turned and as she did, Michael was there just in time to catch her, as she fell to the floor in a dead faint.

Michael, realising it for what it was, treated it accordingly and helped his love recover as quickly as he could.

"Vena, sweetheart - what is wrong? Whyever did you faint? Are you ok... are you pregnant? Oh my, are you pregnant?" Michael was beside himself.

"Sshhh no, no I am not," established Vena. "I am overworked and very tired. I don't know what came over me, I think I forgot to eat lunch today too."

Michael suddenly felt deflated. Vena saw his face

and it was at that moment that she realised, there were times when the saying 'blood is thicker than water' doesn't always apply.

She felt more for this man than she had ever felt for her brother, her mother, or her father. Not that it mattered. She knew her parents were dead, and didn't give that a second thought, though she had at least seen to their burial on her return from just burying her aunt. They had sent her there to make sure that when she passed, she was buried in the old ways. This had also kept her safe.

Vena had thought her brother to be dead and yet there he was, alive and well, waiting to be approved by the Alpha of her pack, *The Lupos Pack*, so that he could be a part of it... a part of *her* life.

This was uncomfortable to say the least, she must see him. She needed to discover what his intentions were.

Gavenia rose from her bed. She and Michael had been close last night, and he had been much more gentle than usual. Vena had very much appreciated this as she was feeling tender in body and spirit. She felt that seeing her brother had literally knocked the stuffing out of her.

Michael was already up and about on pack business. So, she showered slowly and thoroughly, allowing the water to wash the thoughts out of her head, meaning she could start the day on a fresh note.

As with most packs, all single males and females over the age of eighteen who had not yet found their mate, ate in the pack house. This pack was no different, with the exception of the age. There was a vast age range as the fewer singles that existed, the less chance there was of meeting your mate at a younger age.

Alpha Michael had employed one of the humans in the pack to be the chef, which was an excellent move on his part. This woman could cook up a storm!

And so, when Gavenia walked down the stairs to the dining hall, not only was she met with the most delicious smell, but also with a very noisy bunch of men and women, chattering and laughing.

As per usual, she and the twins had their own table allocated to them in a small corner, tucked away, but she always greeted the pack first before taking a seat.

The tables were in four long rows, and Shirley was cooking as fast as they could eat. Vena walked the length of each row, and as she approached the final row, she realised there was a guard at the table at the very end.

"*Okay, this is it,*" she said under her breath, and

braced herself to face her brother for the first time in many years.

# CHAPTER 18

## ANGER AND RESENTMENT

Gavenia walked with purpose towards the table where the bald man was eating his breakfast. A mere two feet away stood a guard. She dismissed him with her eyes and looked straight at the man. His strong gaze met hers, and immediately there was recognition.

Vena addressed him, "I shall see you in your room, immediately after eating."

The man nodded in response and bowed as expected, sitting down to continue his meal as Vena walked away. The guard resumed his position.

Michael was doing the training and wouldn't be able to give his attention to the new boy until after lunch. It irked him a little, but this was the way things were. Baldasorre was also busy, and Vena had spoken to him asking if it was appropriate for her visit to be this morning. He wasn't really keen, but he had given the go ahead on the proviso that the guard kept a close eye on them.

So it was that Gavenia walked slowly to the unit that held the man she knew to be her brother.

Teddy was once again on guard and said hello to his Luna as she approached.

"Hi Teddy," she said. "Can you do me a big favour please? I want you to stay here and watch, but I want you to say nothing of what you see. Could you do that for me?"

"Yes," replied Teddy, "of course."

Teddy opened the door and allowed Vena to enter the unit. She walked steadily over the threshold. There before her sat Ciaran.

"Hello Ciaran, my brother, I thought you to be dead, tell me what happened."

"Ha, no hero welcome party for me then," bellowed Ciaran. "Dead! You thought I was dead!" he exclaimed.

"Hush," demanded Vena.

"Hahaha," cried Ciaran. "He doesn't know, does he? He knows nothing at all. Well, well, well... Does he even know you have a brother? Come on sis, tell me, what the hell does he know - just how far can I blow your world apart?"

"Ciaran please," pleaded Vena. "What do you want? My life here is good, you always wanted what I had, just because I got the vampire bloodline, and you didn't. You assumed that as twins we would have identical powers, Ciaran," she said. "We are fraternal twins, *not identical*. You got your own set of powers; you choose how to utilise those."

Gavenia continued to berate her brother. "You were sent away because you would not leave me alone. You constantly bullied me, or has that slipped your mind? And then I was sent away to Aunt Ailith's, when our parents were killed."

"YEAH," Ciaran interrupted, "when *our* parents were killed."

"Again, shush," pushed Vena. "This conversation goes no further. I knew they were dead, and I was being called to them. When I arrived everyone had gone, even *you* Ciaran, and no one had buried them. You couldn't even bury your own parents, Ciaran. Damn you!" growled Gavenia, barely suppressing the wolf within her.

Ciaran jumped up from his seat, making a grab for Gavenia. Teddy headed straight for him in a flash, but not before Ciaran had managed to hiss to Vena...

"They are dead - you might as well have killed them with your own hands, and for that, *you will pay*."

# CHAPTER 19

## MEETINGS

Teddy let out a threatening growl and Ciaran sat down obediently. He knew at this time and location, it was not the right thing to begin a fight; there were too many people around and his fight was not with the pack.

Teddy, having put Ciaran in his place, turned his attention to his Luna "Are you okay, Vena?"

"Yes, yes, thank you Teddy. Please say nothing of what you have seen and heard today. I appreciate your loyalty to me." Teddy nodded towards Vena. He had heard everything that had passed between the two siblings, he would not be repeating it but nor would he be forgetting it. He would, for the future, be wary of this man and felt there was more to him than what he was telling his sister.

The black wolf could feel a shift in the dynamics. He felt that the things in the pack were about to undergo some kind of change, but he was unaware of what or how they might change. He felt frustrated as he was unable to get to his vantage point to view the pack from a safe distance. Worse still, with things as they were, he didn't know how long it would be before he might be able to get there. Patience would have to be his friend for the time being.

Gavenia walked away from Teddy feeling somewhat shaken. Of all the feelings she had expected, to feel shaken was not among them. Vena knew that this was not the end by a long shot. In her wildest dreams she could only imagine what he might be thinking of doing right now. Why now? Her life was so settled, he had always been trouble. She should have been honest from the start; it was too late now.

As these thoughts ran through her mind, she found herself totally distracted and walked right into Baldasorre. He had finished his errands much sooner than he had anticipated, and so was on his way to see Ciaran to establish his usefulness within the pack. Of course, it wasn't just about whether he would be useful, it was about whether they felt he would be trustworthy, and be a loyal warrior, upholding the laws of the pack.

"Vena…" he enquired. "Are you alright?"

"Oh yes," she replied. "I was in a world of my own.

I have just been to visit Ciaran, the young man responsible for breaching our boundary yesterday. It certainly gives one food for thought, what with that and all of my other responsibilities. I find my plate is overflowing right now. I think it might be time to take on someone else for the school duties that have kept me so busy."

At that she walked off, leaving Baldasorre somewhat thoughtful himself.

"So, you say, Ciaran, that your parents are both dead, and that your mate died bearing your pup who died alongside her." Baldasorre probed.

"Yes sir, that is correct," Ciaran retorted.

"From that point you simply carried on walking, looking for somewhere to put down some roots?"

"Again, yes sir, that is correct," replied the rogue boy.

Baldasorre continued with the questioning of

Ciaran for some time. "And you are of vampire bloodline too... can you tell me Ciaran, which is prominent - the wolf, or the vampire?"

"The wolf, sir, but I have been unable to transition since the death of my mate. I feel as if a part of me went with her."

"I see. Then it just remans for Alpha Michael to see you and for the three of us to have a discussion. We will then make a decision about whether we feel you might fit in with the pack."

With that, the Beta walked away.

# CHAPTER 20

## DECISIONS

"Move it," barked Michael as he finished the last of the training schedules. It had been a tough one today. He had a couple of guys that were very good, and they needed to be pushed to their limits for Michael to get the very best out of them.

He was very pleased with the efforts they had given today, and slapped them on the back, thanking and praising them at the same time for how well they had performed.

He went with them to the communal showers and cleaned down, got a quick change of clothes and made a bee line for the unit where Ciaran was being held.

Ciaran had repeated the same story to Michael as he had to Baldasorre. Michael struggled with the story but could not fault it. He had an uneasy feeling but couldn't put his finger on it.

He sent a mind link to Baldasorre and to Gavenia to meet him in his office in one hour. So, one hour later the three sat there with refreshments from Shirley, the chef, discussing the outcome of Ciaran. Michael went first.

"I have heard this story and although I can find no fault with him or a gap within the story, there is something not right. I think he should be thrown out."

Baldasorre was on the fence. On the one hand he agreed that the story had no holes that could be picked at. The man was marked so at some point he had had a mate. He felt the man should be kept close so they could watch him, and wondered what his reason was for being here.

At this point, Vena was unusually quiet and when addressed, she seemed at a loss as to what to say.

"I'm not sure on this one. We have had men, women and families join us in the past and they have seemed easy to read, but this guy is not so easy, and I don't feel comfortable around him. There is something and I'm really not sure. I don't think he should leave but neither do I feel he should stay."

"Vena, honey," began Michael. "This really isn't like you to not have a firm opinion. We will not go ahead with any decision until you can decide. Until then, we will remove him from the unit and place him in the cells. Would you like to visit him again?"

"Yes, I will. I will take the time now and give him just a few moments. I will take Teddy with me, please." Teddy was summoned and the two of them went down to the holding unit. Teddy waited outside, whilst Vena went inside to speak with Ciaran.

Vena spoke up as Ciaran sat on the sofa. "Well dear brother, it seems we have something of a dilemma here. Do you stay, do you go, or do we lock you in a cell?"

In a flash he once again had Gavenia by the throat. Teddy was beside him within seconds, and Vena held up her hand in Teddy's direction.

Ciaran hissed at her, "I'll tell you what will happen; you will let me stay, you will tell them that you think I will be fine, and if you don't, I'll tear your world to shreds. Do you understand me, sister darling?"

There was a pregnant pause. "I said, Do. You. Understand." Gavenia nodded and Ciaran released her, dropping her to the floor.

Immediately, Teddy helped his Luna to regain

her composure.

"Do not push me, Ciaran. You can stay but, *do not push me.* You have what you want for now, but this is far from over." She turned to the exit.

"Teddy, come. Again, I trust you saw nothing?"

"I saw nothing, Vena. I saw and I heard nothing," was the reply as they walked back to the office in the packhouse.

Like before, the black wolf watching covertly could feel a shift like no other. There was a protective barrier forming around the Luna of this pack. He *needed* to get back to his vantage point, and soon.

# CHAPTER 21

## THE NEW BOY

Gavenia walked quietly towards the office door. She was far from happy but knew what had to be done, *at least for now*. She would deal with him in her own time, in her own way, with the help of Teddy. Right now, Teddy was her only ally.

Vena opened the door and threw on a smile as she sat down with the boys.

"Right my lovelies," she said. "My decision is this. Ciaran, I am sure, is hiding something, we are all agreed on that. However, since we are not aware of what and we cannot find any holes in his story, *which as far as we know may be the truth*, it may be that there is just more to his story than we are being told. I propose we let him stay but create a tag team for him... headed up by Teddy. What are your thoughts on this?" Vena hated lying to the most important men in her life but right now she had no choice.

The boys had listened intently, and both agreed that this seemed like a good idea, although they thought that the holding unit was not really an ideal location for him. If he was going to reveal anything, he needed to have more freedom, so he would be given one of the rooms at the side of the packhouse, that housed the single males.

Teddy was housed in this building and so it made sense to put him in the same block as him and move the men around to ensure that everyone in that block of ten men was assigned to the tag team.

Several hours later and Ciaran's room was ready. The whole team was now 'in situ,' and Baldasorre was given the task of addressing the new boy. He took Teddy along with him, so that he could hand him over and get on with his pack duties.

"Well Ciaran, it seems that you will be, for now at least, living as part of the pack. You are to be given a room in block C; this is Teddy's block so if you have any issues, please go to him first. We have here a list of rules that we expect our pack members to adhere to. You will be on a six-month trial, after which, other pack members will be given one month to raise objections as to why they might not want you here. If there are none, you will be given an official welcome ceremony. Again, any issues or questions, see Teddy. I do not wish to be bothered with trivialities. You will of course be assigned a position of work. Luna Gavenia will be in touch with details of that."

Teddy eyed his new companion with suspicion -

he didn't like him, and with good reason.

"Come on then Ciaran, let's go," said Teddy and they slowly walked to the block of flats that Ciaran would call home.

Teddy left him and went to his room, although there was a lack of technology that was to be had from before the great war, a two-way mirror was a great way to keep an eye on him.

# CHAPTER 22

## CIARAN

Ciaran lay down on the bed. This was the most comfort he had felt in some time. Even the bed at the unit could not compare to this. He fell asleep instantly.

When he awoke, he was slightly disorientated, and it took a few moments for him to realise where he was. Once he had gathered his senses, he went to the bathroom to take a shower. On his return, he checked out the rest of the apartment and realised that there were clothes in the wardrobe. *Great, he had clothes.* He just assumed they were for him... they couldn't be for anyone else.

Teddy's shift had ended an hour ago. He had

arranged for one of his close friends to try and get close to Ciaran, although he was still being watched by someone else at the apartment from the other side.

Ciaran jumped at the sound of the door; "Hey hey newbie," shouted the voice. "Open up boy."

Ciaran walked sullenly toward the door. "Hello, what gives?" he said.

"Hi," said this short blond girl, who looked like she couldn't knock the skin off a rice pudding.

"Hi," she repeated. "My name is Blondie," and as she looked up, he stared into the most beautiful, blood-red eyes. "You want some dinner? I'm starving." Blondie laughed the most melodious laugh. He smirked… boy he wouldn't mind a piece of her. Ciaran's eyes drank in the sight of her.

"Err, yeah sure," he spoke. "I'm pretty hungry myself."

The two set off to the pack house. The women with no mates are housed in the first two blocks: A and B.

"There are absolutely no overnight stays, it is one of the pack rules," Blondie informed him. She made straight for the blood bar and raw meat nibbles. Then, moved onto the more social food. They ate together in silence. Ciaran looked up once to see that her eyes were now a beautiful black, *how superbly novel*, he thought.

She then asked if he would like to take a walk around the village to familiarise himself with it, so that when he was given a position, he would at least be a little bit familiar with things.

Blondie took him all around, and wherever they went, there was always someone watching carefully in the shadows. Whilst Blondie was hoping to extricate information from Ciaran, he was looking and thinking up ways to put his plan into action.

He needed to give her the slip and get rid of the idiot that had been following them too. Well, nothing like an old trick.

"Hey, Blondie, I need the toilet. Can I use these here or will they be locked now?"

"Oh no, we never lock them, there's no need. Please go ahead." Ciaran popped straight through the door. He knew he didn't have long. *Yep, a window, straight out the back.* The guy that was following was out front, so no issue there. He slipped out of the window and as he did, he transformed into his wolf and ran as fast as he could... straight into the woods.

# CHAPTER 23

## CIARAN'S PLAN

From his viewpoint, the black wolf watched slyly in silence. The murmur of his pup came from behind him. A low growl sent the pup skittling frightened and cold, back to the rough lair that had become his home and that of his mother's.

His mother lay there in human form, cold and hungry. The black wolf had brought little back from his hunt, only just enough to keep them going for a couple of days. How long would this go on? Although the pup was very young at eighteen months old, he had the maturity of a six-year-old.

The wolf watched. He could see there was some level of panic around the outskirts of the village, and so zoomed in, allowing his special powers to take over. His eyes narrowed and within moments he could very clearly see the scene unfold before his eyes.

There was a small crowd and they appeared to be shouting at a small girl, a blonde girl. She looked upset but she was certainly holding her own. Then, the large man he knew to be the Beta appeared, and he was unsurprised to see him hug the young girl, clearly his daughter.

Ciaran had had his fun. He came out from the woods, dressed in the same clothes he had disappeared in.

"YOU, you damn ape!" shouted Blondie. "How dare you disappear on me like that." She punched and kicked him, showing she was definitely no pushover.

"You have been gone for *ages*, where have you been?"

"Oh, don't you worry about me. I haven't been far, and I was keeping an eye on the show," he laughed. Blondie had taken a dislike to him, but he wasn't here to make friends, far from it. He had only one thing on his mind.

Baldasorre watched the scene and said nothing, but it was there in his mind, and it would not be missed off his report.

With the evening turning sour, he returned to his rooms at the block. Teddy was watching him through the two-way mirror. Something was unsettling him, and he wasn't sure what it was. There was a smell when he came back from his escapades, it was familiar, but faint. He just couldn't quite get it.

Teddy had a very good sense of smell; it was very heightened, but he just could not place this scent. Could it be wolf? *No, Ciaran couldn't transition*, and the smell wasn't strong enough, so, Teddy put it to the back of his mind.

Ciaran showered and went to bed. He was tired, body and mind, and tomorrow would see him working... what a joke.

Gavenia had made the decision to place Ciaran where she could keep an eye on him at all times. He would be helping out at the school; this was the ideal location, not least because Teddy also worked there - he was the head gym instructor.

Gavenia was placing him in the library on the inventory of all the school stock. It was time consuming, and she had better things to do right now. The biggest of which was a meeting with Michael and the girls. It was confession time.

This was not going to be easy for any of them, but it was something that needed to be sorted and sooner rather than later, as the girls' birthday was looming, and their full powers would be gifted to them.

Vena also wanted Michael to marry her that day, as some of the non-humans had adopted the human ways as time had gone by, and a marriage ceremony was one of them. However, they preferred the binding and jumping of the brush version to the biblical version.

And so, it was for the next few months that Ciaran would quietly sit in the library, sorting stock and doing his inventory, formulating his plan.

# CHAPTER 24

## CONFESSION

The twins and Vena sat around the table in Alpha Michael's office. The pack had come a long way in the ten years since Michael had found the twins, and even further since his beautiful Luna, Gavenia, had come into his life.

His back was facing them, and he was staring out of the window, watching the world go by. He loved everything he saw, and was a happy man, life was good.

What was it that had brought his little family to him at this time? He had long since given up on the idea of his own children as the years had passed, and he and Vena had not been blessed. Michael turned around and looked fondly at them and took his seat. Shirley had just delivered some delicious fresh scones with jam and tea.

"So, my wonderful girls, what can I do for you today? Who is to go first?"

"Well…" started Hala, boldly, "Aremis and I have been holding out on you Papa Alpha. I know that you are aware that we are witches, but there is so much more to the two of us than just that. We were bound by our parents to not reveal anything until we were fourteen, and we now need to tell you the whole truth of our birth rights."

"Oh, I see," said Michael. "Well of course, I always knew there was more to you than just me finding you. However, just what, I had no idea. So please, go ahead."

From then on, the girls began their tale, right up to the present day.

"So, papa, here we are at almost fourteen and nearing the day when we will gain our full powers. We won't know for sure how they will affect us but, we have the coven, and we have Vena, who has been doing some extensive research into fae history and how their powers will manifest."

Initially, Michael was angry and demanded to have Hilda and Baldasorre in the room immediately. The two came running. Of course, Baldasorre knew nothing of what had been going on. Hilda immediately sat everyone down and explained that Fae was not to be feared, it was something that needed to be harnessed and treated with respect. It was a valuable, useful tool.

She took the time to explain about the elements that had been given to the girls, and how they might be able to utilise them, to help the pack.

Michael was astounded, not least by the fact that

they had fae blood, but that Vena had known all this time and said nothing.

He looked at her and she looked back. "Michael, this was not my secret to tell."

"No Vena, of course not, but nevertheless I might have been able to help. Still, I'm glad you had Hilda. You must not keep secrets Vena, you are my mate. There is nothing that we cannot overcome together...So, what next?" asked Michael. *He had taken this very well*, thought Vena, now for the bombshell!

"The girls of course must have a party. Their powers come at midnight and that is when they will go to the coven and Hilda and the witches will take over."

"Well, yes, of course." Michael approved of this and Gavenia was pleased that so far everything was going to plan, because she was about to shake him up just a little.

"Err Michael…"

"Yes?"

"I guess it's my turn now. Alpha Michael James Mckenzie, *would you marry me?*"

Michael shot up from his chair, almost upending the tea and what was left of the scones. The girls screamed with delight, then everything went quiet while Vena and the girls waited with bated breath to see what Michael's response would be.

"YES, yes, of course," he said, gathering Vena up in his arms and squeezing her tightly.

"Hey, hey, Michael - not so tight… I want to marry you so that our pup isn't born outside of marriage!

# CHAPTER 25

## TEDDY

The squeals and shouts could be heard all over the village, and Baldasorre was one of the first to offer congratulations to the four of them. This was quickly followed by Hilda and the rest of the pack that was in the house at that time.

News spread fast and before you knew it, the whole village knew about the pregnancy, the marriage, and the party.

Michael was ecstatic; the two of them had waited so long to be parents, he felt an overwhelming urge to protect his Luna, Vena. He didn't want to let her out of his sight, it had been bad enough before, but now, how was he going to cope?

*Teddy*, that was the answer. He would take him off Ciaran's watch and place him with Vena. Teddy was young; he was twenty-one and had yet to find his mate. This was an issue with so many of the young men and women. Simply due to the fact that they were an isolated pack and relied on new members joining, or their current members going out on what could only be described as pilgrimages, to search for lone people or small groups to come join the pack. This brought new blood into the pack and allowed members to find mates.

Teddy was more than happy to be assigned to Vena. He knew his Alpha had great faith in him as a warrior, in spite of his youth.

Teddy was a werewolf and a damn strong one at that. He worked out a lot and his recent training had obviously paid off. Michael had noticed him training, he had seen how hard he had worked in the gym and how he coached the younger members, be they wolves, humans, or any other species of the pack.

Teddy always saw to it that everyone got a fair fight and showed humans how to best the others if they were ever under attack. This was an aspect that even Michael had not thought of. Michael knew that Teddy was trustworthy, and that Vena would be safe in his hands, and so it was that Gavenia and Teddy became one.

Where there was Teddy, there was Vena, and where there was Vena, there was Teddy.

Teddy and Vena ran as wolves through the woods. This was rare for Vena as she mostly only ever ran with Michael in her wolf form, but Vena was finding she needed to stretch out more and more lately.

Teddy had the reddest of hair and the deepest

brown eyes, and today was one of the days when the two would run.

The noise of bones cracking was deafening as the two transitioned to their wolves. Teddy's wolf was large with thick, red fur and solid muscle. He went by the name of Derry, meaning Red Oak. He certainly lived up to that - he was solid as an oak tree.

Vena, although a tall wolf, was not as big as Teddy, who stood a good few inches above her, and the once slender wolf of Vena was slightly thicker set than before, due to the pregnancy no doubt.

The two ran for some time, until Teddy picked up the familiar smell that he recalled from some weeks previous. He could not place it, no matter how he tried. It was there in his memory but would not come to the fore.

There was a small lake close to the pack boundary

and they both decided to have a quick dip before making their way back to the village.

Teddy had not been to this particular lake for some time but as soon as he entered it, he knew instantly where the smell was from. The water, it had a very distinctive smell to it. Teddy didn't know why, but logged it in his memory and would ask the sorcerers or the witches on his return.

# CHAPTER 26

## INFORMATION

On their return, Gavenia went to Michael and the girls. There was never a time now that she was ever alone. Although Ciaran was still formulating his plan, the fact that she was never alone was very frustrating for him. He couldn't get close enough to threaten or chip away and make her life miserable. He was running out of patience.

Meanwhile, the black wolf was also frustrated. The shift in the dynamics of the pack had upset him; he also couldn't find the balance he needed to get to where he could reach his vantage point and view the pack once more. It had been too long. He needed to see his mate and pup. They needed to be fed, and to know that he was still there, and they were in his thoughts.

Teddy had left Vena safely with Michael, and he was now on his way to see Hilda or Samuel.

Samuel was head of the sorcerers and slightly intimidating, so he was hoping to see Hilda first, but he lucked out.

"Alright Samuel?" questioned Teddy. "I have come to you with a problem that I'm hoping you might be able to help me with."

Samuel stood before him, a mere three feet tall, casually dressed, and just staring. He was the scariest person Teddy knew.

"Well?" the voice boomed from the little man.

"Err, yes...," said Teddy. "I've been smelling this smell, err, no, well what I mean..."

"For the sake of the Moon Goddess, spit it out boy," cried Samuel.

"Damn it, you're so impatient, give me a break!" yelled Teddy, suddenly finding some courage. "Right, several times I have had this scent waft around me. It felt strangely familiar, and I wouldn't call it unpleasant, but neither would I say I liked it. So today, Luna and I were swimming in the lake by the border and the scent was in the water itself.

"What is it?"

"That's what I need to know and why would I be smelling it elsewhere?"

"Well, that particular lake, I discovered, has an unnecessary amount of zinc in it. It will give off a strange smell but, Teddy I have to say, your sense of smell must be very good to detect that away from the lake itself.

*Yes*, thought Teddy, and now he had to think where he had smelled it and who, if anyone, it had been on.

*Yes that was it, it had been on Ciaran when he had come back from the woods. That must mean he hadn't really been up to much, mind, that's a long way to have gone from the village area where he had disappeared if he was without a wolf. It would've taken at least three hours to have walked that distance and then another three to walk back again. Unless there was another area in the woods that was rich in zinc.* No possibilities should be ruled out yet. It was only fair to get as much information as possible.

The wolf loomed in the darkness. He could see Luna and Teddy as they ran back towards the village. He had brought much food with him this time. He had taken the time to hunt properly before coming back to the lair. He knew he wouldn't be able to risk coming back too soon again and if he did, he would have to bring plenty of supplies.

His mate was looking better, and his pup was too. This pleased him; he hated them both but as mate and father, he didn't want them dead. To him they were an Albatross around his neck. He needed her healthy anyway as he needed her skills.

Soon very soon...

# CHAPTER 27

## PREPARATIONS

Ciaran's preparations were coming along just nicely. He had kept his head down and had annoyed no one, he had no enemies but no friends either. He had figured this to be the best way. He felt *invisible*, he was not of course and was still being watched, though the guards were becoming complacent.

He had earned himself a run for an hour a day and was building muscle in the gym. His daily run was of course with his wolf.

It was amazing that one of his powers was that he could transition, and he never smelled of wolf, so no one would be any the wiser.

It was just after his daily run when he was walking

back to the block, and he passed Teddy.

"Where have you been?" asked Teddy, inhaling deeply. He could smell the zinc, but there was definitely nothing to suggest wolf on Ciaran. The zinc smell was strong today, as if he too had been swimming in it.

"Just for my daily jog," replied Ciaran. Teddy eyed him suspiciously, but let it go and walked on to finish his business for the day. A mental note was made to watch Ciaran more closely.

Ciaran turned as Teddy walked away. Had he underestimated this man? He didn't think so, but then again, perhaps he should make some changes to his plans.

Hala and Aremis were having dress fittings for being bridesmaids. The dresses would double up as party dresses for later in the day, when the girls had their party. At the same time, Gavenia was being fitted for her wedding dress. She was choosing cake decorations for the wedding and for the girls. She was picking flavours and flowers and there were tears and tantrums. It was so stressful that Hilda and Shirley had to come in and break it up.

Shirley was a good sort, *for a human*. She was a bustler. In no time at all, she had the food side of things in order. It was just the cakes that remained. It was Gavenia's wedding cake, and the twins' this time. The girls wanted one each to represent their individual elements and their own personalities. Although they had remained close, their personalities now set them apart and they had started to take their lessons in fae witchcraft separately, *with the exception of one*. In this one, they were learning to use their powers in conjunction with each other.

Shirley began with the wedding cake, drawing on

scraps of paper to give Vena an idea of what she might do. It wasn't long before they agreed to a design and Shirley moved to the girls. They proved to be difficult, and arguments followed, so Shirley threw down her towel and told them straight - **she** was the cook, and **she** would do the design and that was the end of it!

Like it or lump it.

Of course, while this brought laughter from Vena and Hilda, the teenage girls became sullen.

Preparations, it seems, were not as easy as they all thought...

# CHAPTER 28

## THE WEDDING

In no time at all, it was the eve of the wedding and also the eve of the girls fourteenth birthday. Gavenia could not have been happier. Her suspicions of her brother were at the back of her mind; her thoughts were filled with that of the upcoming nuptials and the birthday celebrations.

She, Michael, and the rest of the pack wouldn't be a part of the coven's celebrations for Hala and Aremis. That was a private, intimate gathering and more of an initiation ceremony. Anyone that wasn't part of the coven would not be in attendance.

And so, alone in her private quarters, Gavenia allowed herself to sleep.

The pack house had been decorated beautifully, and everyone was in attendance. Teddy was giving Vena away and as they approached the large open doors of the house with the two girls behind them, everyone gasped at the beauty that was Gavenia. Even Ciaran, was taken aback by the aura that surrounded her.

Ten witches were ahead of them with their broomsticks in the air criss-crossed, and Hilda at the head.

As Vena approached, Hilda banged her broom on the floor three times, sending sparkles into the air. The broom left her hand and lay on the floor at the feet of Michael.

Michael held in his hand a red ribbon and a white ribbon; one to tie the heart and one to tie the mind, and then they would together jump the brush.

As they made their promises to each other and

tied the ribbons, the broom sparkled as if it was filled with electricity. This done, they both jumped the broom, and as they did, the broom flew up into the air with orbs of light, sparkles, and flower petals flying in all directions.

Hilda had done a great job with that spell.

Hala and Aremis had been absolutely delighted to be the flower girls. Their birthday celebrations would come after the wedding, and both of them were very happy to be taking second place.

With the whole village being a part of the celebrations, there would be only a skeleton guard on the boundary. This had been decided some time ago, and although nothing had been said to anyone, it had been almost a given.

The black wolf was feeling happy… everything was

now in place. It wouldn't be long now until he could make his move. His mate was looking healthier, the pup was just a burden, but he had to tolerate him as he needed the woman he called mate.

"Agatta," he growled towards his mate. "The time is almost upon us, we will soon be moving on. Prepare."

With that he was gone.

Everyone was eating and the band was playing. Michael and Vena had already had the first dance and the day was moving along. They had all agreed that the wedding would officially end at five o'clock and birthday celebrations would take over.

After a quick change of clothes into something more comfortable, Vena came down the back stairs with Teddy, as ever when not with Michael, to rejoin the festivities.

She was already flagging and knew that she would definitely not make it through the night, as would most of the guys, including Michael.

Vena made it to eleven forty-five at night, when everyone sang the happy birthdays to the girls, and they were carried away to their separate areas in the woods that had been prepared by the coven. Teddy walked her to her room.

"Would you like me to help you any further, Vena?" he offered.

"No thank you," was the reply and she entered the room, closing the door behind her.

# CHAPTER 29

## HALA AND AREMIS

Gavenia was shattered. She knew that it would some time before Michael got here; they had stopped their love making the minute he knew she was in pup as he did not want to risk losing something so precious. She also knew that Teddy would have reported straight to him that she was safe in their quarters.

Vena went to the bathroom, showered, and put on her favourite joggers and loose fit top. She walked from the dressing room towards the bed and as she rounded the corner, she was hit right in the face by what seemed like a brick wall.

That was the last thing she knew.

Hala was sat inside a circle with a small moat surrounding her. It was midnight and the water in the moat was restless, as if it was waiting for instruction. Outside of the circle was one sorcerer and five witches. Hilda would be alternating between both Hala and Aremis, to make sure nothing got too much out of control.

Hala had been slowly working on her powers over the last few years but now she had the full ability and force to really let go. She looked at the water in the moat and listened to what the witches asked of her; it was a test as much as anything to see that she could harness the powers she had been given and not allow them to run loose over the forest around them.

"Make the water grow in volume, Hala," said the

first witch. Hala concentrated and closed her eyes. She began to feel warm, and a blue glow formed around her. The water slowly rose to the very top of the moat and as it did so, Hala exhaled, and the blue glow faded.

"Well done, Hala," congratulated the witch. The second which began; "now raise the water to form a wall around you."

Hala, at this point feeling confident, got a little carried away and raised one side and flooded the other.

"Hala!" scolded the sorcerer. "Concentrate, this is serious. You can do a lot of damage. Now do the wall and do it *right*."

Hala set to and the wall of water rose gently up to the top of her head as she glowed blue and then went gently down as her aura faded.

"Much better Hala. Well done," the third witch

said to her. "Now this time when you raise the wall, bring it over your head and make it into a twister."

Hala had to attempt this three times before she could get control of the water, needless to say, she was wet. Eventually, it was done.

The fourth witch ordered, "I want you to make a water ball and throw it through the air." Hala seemed to be able to get the drift of this one fairly easily and was throwing balls of water over the forest until the water in the moat was no more.

"Brilliant, Hala. There is one more task to do and that will be done with Aremis."

Aremis was sat in a circle of stones, her tests very much the same as Hala's. Her first one was to double the number of seedlings, which she managed easily, then to make them grow in a wall around her. Aremis was so much more focused than Hala.

Aremis didn't like to make the vines twist around each other, she felt it made them look ugly, but she did it, nevertheless.

The next test for Aremis was to make flower puffs. These were like huge balls of flower seeds that when thrown, would make the recipient sneeze and cough.

The sorcerers and Hilda explained to both the girls that there would be so much more to their powers than what they had just done, these were mere games compared to what they would learn over the next few years. There was one little test to be had now though, if they were both up for it.

Both girls sat together back-to-back, and Hilda instructed Aremis to throw irritating seedlings throughout the air that would make everyone sneeze, whilst Hala must make it rain to dampen the seedlings rid the area of them.

Both girls concentrated, their eyes closed as their auras surrounded the two of them. The colours mixed, making a rainbow of lovely colours, that became brighter and brighter. Seedlings began to float through the air and as they did, the colours became more vibrant, and more seedlings appeared.

No rain, no rain at all. Everybody sneezed - they could see the concentration on the faces of the girls, but no rain, when suddenly, the pair vanished!

# CHAPTER 30

## MISSING

The downpour was torrential, and with the rain, both girls were back almost as quickly as they had gone. The sorcerers looked at each other, *they just teleported.*

Aremis is the stronger one, and Hala cannot make it rain over her sister as she is casting; they must be apart.

"Where did you go, girls?"

"I went east..." said Aremis

"...and I went west," continued Hala. "The odd thing is, though it was just a second, I'm sure I saw a black wolf. I could have been mistaken, but I don't think so."

It was two-thirty in the morning and the festivities were coming to a close. Michael was ready to retire and having said his thank yous and goodbyes, he turned his attention to thoughts of Gavenia and bed.

Walking slowly but steadily towards the room, he rubbed the spot on his forehead and nose that had been hurting him since earlier on in the evening. He had had a fair few ales, so thought perhaps his senses were playing tricks on him, and that, although he was tightly linked to Vena and could feel her pain, it was nothing to do with her.

He was halfway up the steps to their quarters, and he knew he was wrong... the pain had intensified. He ran the rest of the way.

As he burst through the door, he knew before he

even got in the room that she wasn't there. Michael was bereft; his wolf came out immediately. Ezra was screaming and howling for Paz and Vena. There was no smell here, no smell at all, only Vena's scent. Where was she? Where had she gone? Why and who with?

Baldasorre was at his side immediately, he switched to his bat form and went out to survey the area. He looked everywhere and found *nothing*.

Night turned to day and the whole of the Lupus pack was gathering outside the pack house. Michael was like a bear with a sore head; he was angry, he was hurt, he was only half of a whole. He felt like he couldn't address the pack at that moment and handed over the reins to Baldasorre and Teddy.

Baldasorre addressed the pack.

"Our Luna Gavenia is missing. We do not know as of yet if she has left or has been taken. However, we are working on the assumption that she has been taken. The first step will be to search the grounds thoroughly, leaving no stone unturned. We will then go outside the border and assess any evidence that we have and take steps from that point on. Teddy will be leading the search and will break it down into search parties."

Hala was first to come forward with what she had seen the previous night. Teddy logged this with other bits that came to light, like footprints, and there was also a chunk of black fur. It looked like he may have lost his balance, as if he was carrying something heavy and caught himself on the briars.

The search continued but turned up nothing more than what they already had.

Michael had been trying to mind link Vena, but he could not get through to her at all. He felt that she was not dead but in danger. He was so grateful for

Teddy and Baldasorre, however it did not stop him from taking it out on them. They knew what he was going through and took it on the chin.

He walked across the bedroom and picked up one of her scarves, smelling her fragrance,

Michael fell to his knees and cried.

# CHAPTER 31

## KIDNAPPED

The black wolf was powerful, and he had worked hard to make sure he was strong enough to lift the Luna in his jaw and throw her around his neck so that he could run easier.

Taking her had been easy, so much simpler than at first thought. It was the getting away that had proved difficult.

What had seemed like a nice easy run was turning into something of a nightmare. He easily made it to the edge of the forest unnoticed as everyone was busy celebrating. He had not anticipated the after party of the girls' powers. He was hit by a water ball several times, and to sneeze quietly was quite a feat.

Just when the black wolf thought it was over, it rained down seedlings. He sneezed endlessly, catching him by surprise. He slipped into the briars and caught his fur; *damn that hurt*, the little stabs were always the worst. And then the downpour came, and he left his footprints in the mud.

He was fuming at this as it showed not only that he had been there, but that he was carrying something by the depth of his print.

Once he was over the boundary, the rain was no more, and the earth was not soft - there would be no prints and no scent to follow.

The black wolf headed towards his mate who was waiting at the entrance to the silver mine. The black wolf had spent some time here and had prepared a little cell of silver and wolfsbane, especially for the lovely Luna.

The wolf dropped Gavenia at Agatta's feet. She

dragged her into the cell, not flinching once as she touched the silver for, she was one of the rare wolves that silver didn't affect. She had prepped a drink with wolfsbane in it and forced it down the semiconscious Gavenia. This would not kill her but would render her wolf useless.

Agatta had removed any and all silver from around the rest of the lair they now lived in and closed the cell off. She had placed a boundary of silver around them as a protective barrier. Agatta hoped this would be enough for now, at least until her mate had done whatever he intended, and they could move onto a proper life as promised.

He had promised so much, so many times.

Gavenia was beginning to stir. Her head was fuzzy, and it ached; she was thirsty, very thirsty. She saw a table with a jug of water and a cup on it, noticing that she was on a makeshift bed in a cell of silver. Gavenia wasn't cold. The air down there was relatively warm, and besides, she had her jog suit on. Whoever had put her there had also given her a rough blanket.

"Ooohhhhh," she groaned, as she moved her head. This had to be the work of Ciaran. She decided to lay and listen for a while. All she could hear was a woman and a child, which baffled her. How could this be Ciaran? But who else would want to harm her?

She turned over, and there lay a huge black wolf. He had been there the entire time, staring at her, and she couldn't smell him.

The black wolf stood up and padded around the cell, careful not to touch the silver bars and as he did so, his bones began to crack as he transitioned back to his human form.

There before her stood her twin brother, Ciaran.

# CHAPTER 32

## TRUTHS

"So, here we are Vena, my little sis. Now let's have a wee chat, shall we?"

"There is nothing that you and I have to talk about," spat Vena. "You will be caught whether I live or die. You *will* be caught, and you *will* pay the price."

"Ah but there is so much we have to talk about Vena, isn't there..." he said very quietly, Gavenia turned her back.

"TURN AROUND," he bellowed. Vena shivered; she knew how threatening he could be, but refused to do his bidding.

"Agatta. Get in here," he demanded. At his

command, this petite woman came running through the door. Vena turned and was instantly horrified by what she saw.

"Ciaran, you took her in your wolf form, how could you do that? Is she your mate?"

"Oh yes, she is my mate. I never lost her in birthing." Agatta looked towards Gavenia. Suddenly, she realised that what she had been told by Ciaran was not the truth, this woman was not the evil twin sister that Ciaran had made her out to be. Vena returned the look with something that resembled compassion, as she surveyed the scars on the face and the neck of Agatta. Vena could only imagine what other scars lay beneath the rags that passed as clothing.

"Look at me, bitch," shouted Ciaran with venom. "I want to know why and how our parents got killed. Tell me and tell me now. I was there Gavenia. Why did no one else die? Why just them? We all slept, whoever did that could have killed us all and you know the truth… I know you know the truth!"

"Why would I know the truth?" asked Gavenia. "What the hell would it have to do with me?"

"I'll tell you why, but you know already don't you? Because before we were going to attack, you spoke to them and the attack was rearranged, you damn well know it. Why Vena… why did they change the day?!"

"Why would I know?" shrieked Vena, refusing to reply, knowing that once he had his answer, she could kiss her life goodbye. It was all about holding out for as long as possible.

Gavenia had tried to get in touch with her wolf, but Paz was not responding. She knew that she had been given some wolfsbane, she had drank some water too, and it had made her feel woozy. She was desperate for rest.

Ciaran stormed from the room in a rage.

As she drifted off into a deep sleep, she heard the voice of Agatta whispering in her ear… *'help me get away from him and I'll help you get back to the pack, don't drink the water. It has wolfsbane in it.'*

Teddy knew he had to approach his Alpha with caution and chose to do it with Baldasorre as protection.

"Alpha, it has been a whole twenty-four hours since our Luna went missing, and I have much to tell you."

Baldasorre sat between them, he was ready for the fall out that was about to come. Teddy went over the story regarding Vena and Ciaran, and though it wasn't his to tell, he missed nothing out. He spoke about the smell of zinc, the lakeside from where it came, then moving onto the black wolf and the fact that the girls had caught a glimpse, the footprints, and the tuft of hair.

Baldasorre suddenly looked up. "Did you say black wolf?"

"Yes, why?" said Teddy.

"Well, I could've sworn when we first came here that I caught a glimpse in my peripheral vision but cast it aside."

Michael had sat thus far in silence, when erratically, he jumped from his chair and began throwing everything he could get his hands on.

"SHE LIED! WHEN I FIND HER, BY THE MOON GODDESS SHE WILL PAY..."

Michael knew as soon as he said it that it wasn't true. He loved Gavenia so much and the words were spoken out of anger because he felt she should have confided in him. He could have protected her. Now she was out there somewhere with that fool of a brother, for whatever reason he had no idea, and she was carrying his pup which made it all the worse.

At all costs, *she must be found.*

# CHAPTER 33

## THE SEARCH

The search party knew where to start, thanks to the girls and Teddy. Off to the west towards the lake, on the edge of the boundary.

The footprints left the boundary where the lake began, suggesting that he had swam through the lake and exited somewhere along the bank.

The pack had all crossed the lake now, and began the walk around the far edge to track for footprints that might show where he had come out onto the bank. As it turns out, he had barely swum at all, more like a little paddle. It appeared that he had climbed right out at the far side. But almost instantly the footsteps had disappeared.

Michael was due to join the search party soon, but for now he was tracing the black wolf's movements from the bedroom, through the forest and towards the lake, to see if he could pick up anything at all. The girls were with him; he could smell Vena but nothing else.

It concerned him greatly that he could not communicate with her. It must be wolfsbane that was preventing her wolf from coming to the fore, although she had vampire talents, she may not be able to use those. It was her wolf that held most of her power. The vampire gave her some special powers, but he wasn't aware of what they really were, as she hadn't had any reason to use them. He hoped whatever they were, they would be of use to her.

Michael joined the search party approximately two miles from the western side of the boundary.

He didn't feel anything; his gut feeling was that they needed to be more towards the north. This was more of an intuition rather than a definite knowledge thing.

Hala and Aremis agreed that they too had strong inclinations that north was the direction they should be headed in. The less that Vena drank, the clearer her head became, and the clearer her head became, the more definite her family were in their beliefs that this was the way that she had come.

Michael knew her scent had been compromised in some way, so it was difficult to track. He would not give up. He sat the men down to regroup and have a chat to them.

They decided on four groups that would cover North West, North, North East and the fourth group would spread out and just cover the ground behind, hoping to pick up any clues the others might have missed.

"Between NW and N was the old silver mine. Is anyone covering that area independently?" asked Teddy.

"Good point, Teddy" replied Michael, "you cover the mine and put the fourth group on the NE which was your area."

The search began with new vigour. They were walking steadily towards their designated areas and Teddy was approximately five miles from the silver mine.

*The clock was ticking.*

The search party was aware of the time they had, and Ciaran was also aware that his time with Vena was limited. He needed to move fast if he wanted to get the information out of her that he wanted. He had to make his move while she was weak with the wolfsbane.

# CHAPTER 34

## BATTLE OF WILLS

Ciaran came to the cell to get his sister to finally admit the truth of what had happened. When he came from behind the door that separated his lair and the cell, he was shocked to see a levitating Gavenia surrounded by a foggy type of mist...

"I'm meditating by levitating dear, we vampires often do it - not that you would know that," she said and opened her eyes to reveal blood red. She was hungry for blood and needed to eat, and this was often the best time for what she was about to do.

"Well brother dear, look at me, or can't you? you want the truth, don't you?" He looked straight into her eyes, the red of her iris drawing him in, locking him into a state of hypnosis. A few more seconds and Ciaran would be out of it for at least two hours.

"Agatta, Agatta," called Vena. "Come quickly."

Agatta also came around the door to see Ciaran sleeping soundly and somewhat uncomfortably, in a state of hypnosis. She quickly unlocked the cell and the two of them went through the door to go outside. Before doing so, Agatta went to pick up a small child.

"Oh lord, the child, I forgot about the child. He will hold us up considerably," exclaimed Vena. "Quickly, we must go." And they both ran without further thought into the open air.

"I must do something before we go."

"Can't it wait?" whined Vena.

"No," came the snappy reply. "I must do it now… Ciaran Julius Allanach, I reject you as my mate."

At that moment, three things happened. Teddy

came up from behind to see the three sorry looking figures and Michael came from the left. They both saw and heard them simultaneously. The rejection of Ciaran woke him from his hypnotic slumber, and he roared in pain and anger at being thwarted. He felt the pain of rejection like no other, whereas Agatta felt nothing. It had died the moment he had beat her.

Ciaran ran out from the mine to see the two women, the child, Michael, and Teddy. The pack not far away came for the child and took him to safety.

"It's time for the truth, Gavenia," said Ciaran, slimily.

"This is the one and only time I will ever agree with that goddess forsaken mutt," mumbled Michael.

The girls were also present now, the rest of the

pack moving back for privacy. But not so far that any harm would come to their Alpha or Luna. Gavenia fell to her knees.

"Michael I am truly sorry for the loss of your family, your parents, and pack. I knew my own father and mother were fighting for territory and were about to attack your pack, but I couldn't let them, not that day. You were there, and I had seen you; I knew you to be my true mate. My parents had always favoured Ciaran, they had spoiled him. They sent him away for special training, telling me it was because he bullied me, but I knew the truth. So, I asked them for one thing, and they agreed... they wouldn't attack if you were there. You returned, to see everything you had ever known gone, and the pack responsible for your loss still there sleeping, *even the damn guards*. You took your revenge though, didn't you Michael? I know that you killed my parents. I know that, because my filthy piece-of-work brother left them to rot where they died, and I had to bury them. And because you had to sneak away like a thief in the night - you were unable to bury yours.

Michael, I buried your parents for you too."

# CHAPTER 35

## TOO LATE FOR SORRY

Ciaran just looked at her with hatred. It was clear he still blamed her for their death; she had wanted to save the life of one man and in doing so, she may as well have murdered their parents. That was his view.

He sprang up, changing to wolf mid-air and as he did so, Teddy, who was nearest, did the same.

Teddy's wolf, Derry, was so powerful and majestic. He flipped the black one with his paw and grabbed his throat, all in one swift movement, draining his life source from him. As Ciaran changed back to his human form and lay dying, he cast an almost sorrowful look toward Agatta, and she responded with a sad and somewhat regretful look of her own. As she turned back to face Vena, she thought of the damage he had done and knew that it was *too late for sorry*.

Meanwhile to the side of Agatta, Teddy was having serious problems controlling Derry. All he could smell was fresh spring flowers and it was driving him crazy. Agatta on the other hand, was feeling slightly giddy as her wolf, Alba, was smelling fresh oak and oranges. They turned to face each other, and, in an instance, they knew they had found their mate... their true, forever mate.

Teddy was overwhelmed with pain at the scars on Aggie's face, but he walked towards her and stroked her gently, before kissing the face he instantly loved. Alba and Derry were rapidly soothed, and a calmness fell over the two of them.

Sadly, amidst the devastating blow that had been

dealt to Michael and Vena, the two of them suppressed their energies as this was simply not a time for celebration.

Hala and Aremis were devastated; they didn't know how to comfort their adopted parents. There had to be a way forward for them.

Michael felt tortured with the pain and knowledge that he had killed Vena's parents but also that Vena's parents had slaughtered his whole family. How would they come back from this one?

It had been four and a half months since they had all stood facing one another outside the mine. An uneasy feeling had settled over the Lupos Pack. Everything went on as normal, but nothing felt the same; no one smiled and laughed as before, there were no light-hearted conversations, no one saw their Luna, the Alpha was just that, the Alpha. There was nothing behind his eyes. It was plain for everyone to see that he was a man in great pain... there was no doubt that Luna Gavenia was feeling exactly the same, whether they could see her or not.

Vena sat on the bed, the bed she had shared with Michael right up until the incident at the mine. She cried. She seemed to do nothing but cry. Vena stood to go to the shower, feeling heavy and tired with the pup as it moved constantly inside her.

Reaching for the towel, she stepped out of the shower. Simultaneously, her waters broke. Vena, already wet from the shower didn't notice, but the water gathered beneath her feet, causing her to slip and fall right across the bathroom floor.

Vena let out a blood curdling scream as the first contraction hit, just before her head hit the wall, rendering her unconscious.

# CHAPTER 36

## REGRETS

Michael was out and about on pack business; he had let things drop. Baldasorre had taken over many of his duties along with his two sons who had recently come of age and were keen to be a part of the pack. Now, many people make the assumption that vampires are deadly creatures that kill humans and that is that; they cannot breed, and they are lone creatures that only come out at night.

This is for books and children's nightmares. Vampires drink blood, yes that is true, but invariably they don't practise on humans these days.

They can breed, but only grow to the age of twenty-one. At this age they will find a mate, they are not drawn to someone by a bond like the wolves are, but they do mate for life.

Knowing the pack was in safe hands, Michael had let the reins go a little. He was trying to go back in time. He wanted to forgive, but he couldn't. He didn't know why, but he was trying so hard to get past this thing that was eating into his very soul.

He was at the edge of the wood and was going to go for a run. He stripped and tied his joggers to his leg, and with a huge leap, began his transformation to his beautiful caramel wolf, Ezra.

Michael could not have been more than mid leap when his body stopped and crumpled to the floor in a heap. He was in agony, belly cramped and his head, hell, *his head hurt.*

*'Gavenia, oh Moon Goddess, please let her be alright.'* Michael was feeling every single little twinge. He ran in his human form back to the pack house as

fast as he could.

He made his way straight to the hospital wing, knowing that he would find her there, and there she was. He crumpled before her, begging forgiveness and she to him.

Wave after wave of pain consumed Vena and it went on for hours. She was exhausted. Michael was beside himself.

"Is there anything we can do?" he asked the doctor, and the doctor replied that if it was to continue for much longer, he would intervene and consider performing a caesarean, but only if absolutely necessary. Doctor Peppercorn assured Michael that the pup as yet was not in any distress and was strong, *his concern was for Vena.*

Michael went for a breather as the doctor said there was little he could do, and nothing was happening for the next hour.

Hala and Aremis recalled the day many years ago when they sorted out their Luna, while Michael was out of the way, and they carefully sneaked into the room, and began casting their spells around Vena. They were chanting and working together.

"Let's get this natural, girl," said Aremis, who had turned into the leader out of the two. "Cast me a pool of nice warm water and I'll surround it with natural earth." No sooner was this said than done, the two of them levitated - Vena from the bed as she placed her swollen naked body into the pool.

Almost immediately, Vena felt refreshed and ready to push with renewed vigour.

"Where is Michael?" she cried, and as if on cue he walked right in.

"Wow," he gulped. "Girls, this is fantastic!" He looked at Vena's tired face but could see that she was ready to start again; he could feel the contractions begin again but this time it felt different. He knew that his pup was going to come into the world, and sure enough, with a few good pushes he was there, ready to face his papa.

"A son... my beautiful Luna, you have given me a son. I love you *so very* much..."

# CHAPTER 37

## BALANCE RESTORED

Luna Gavenia was recovering well; her colour was returning, and she was managing to feed the baby herself, although she did have an incredible thirst for blood.

Sat next to her was Alpha Michael. He was gently cradling his son as they prepared to present him to the pack. This was a major event - more so than the wedding, for his son would be the new Alpha when the time came.

The introduction to the pack was akin to a christening in the world now gone. The two of them had talked long into the night, just a few days after his birth to decide his name and had finally chosen one that would be acceptable to them both, and hopefully bring peace and harmony back to the pack.

The sun was out; it was going to be a good day. It was decided to hold the introduction/naming ceremony outside, where there was more room for everyone to see.

Meanwhile, in the village in a little cottage, Teddy was wrapped around his love, Agatta. Neither one of them had ever been so happy. The two had kept a low profile since Agatta had come to the village. There had been no mating ceremony and none of the usual things that would normally go along with meeting your mate.

Agatta's son whom she had borne to Ciaran was almost two, but he was bright. He had to grow up fast. He knew his father had been a bad man and that Derry, Teddy's wolf, had killed him. This didn't matter. Teddy was a kind man and cared deeply for him and for his mother, he too had never felt so happy.

Anwar was now settled in his new home. And Agatta was already expecting a pup with Teddy. The three of them had to be in attendance within the hour so had little time to ready themselves, but ready they were and on their way.

As Shirley stayed in the pack house holding Michaels and Vena's pup, the rest of them made their way out to address the pack.

Michael began his introductions; "Good morning everyone, and welcome. Firstly, I must apologise for not being myself these last few months and hope you understand. Secondly, my apologies must go to Teddy, every one of you must know Teddy. He is my right-hand man when it comes to tracking and training. He is appointed as head of our warriors, and yet, at the time he needed me the most, I wasn't there for him. Teddy, please forgive me, I owe you a mating ceremony to welcome Agatta to the pack. Of course, not forgetting my nephew Anwar."

Teddy and Agatta blushed with embarrassment at being the centre of attention.

"Baldasorre, my close friend and Beta, thank you for allowing me space and time to work through this. I know you are much older than me and wish to take more of a back seat. I understand it is your wish to introduce your two older sons to the pack so they may take over some of your duties and expand their knowledge."

Baldasorre turned and two extraordinarily handsome men walked out of the crowd to the platform, to shake hands with Michael.

"Michael, I give you Bolivar and Silas," exclaimed Baldasorre proudly. Michael heard a gasp to the side of him. It immediately caught the attention of the boys.

Michael laughed and said, "it looked like there would be more than one mating ceremony to be had." The pack laughed along with Bolivar and Silas, much to the girls' embarrassment.

"Apologies and introductions over, it is time to meet my new-born." Shirley walked out and placed his son in the arms of the Luna. There had already been a short, private, naming ceremony in the middle of the night, when the moon was at its fullest and so all that was left was the formalities.

Luna Gavenia passed her son over to Alpha Michael and he raised the boy to the sky.

"I GIVE YOU MY SON, JAMES JULIUS McKENZIE. James was from my father and Julius from Vena's Father, a union we hoped to never separate the two again..."

# THE END